Cup Final

A Comedy

Charles Mander

Samuel French – London
New York – Sydney – Toronto – Hollywood

CHARACTERS

Adjudicator
Sharon
Joe
Martin
Janice
Raymond
Mrs Bland

The action of the play takes place in the dressing room of a converted hall during an Amateur Drama Festival

Time—the present

CUP FINAL

The dressing room of a converted hall during an Amateur Drama Festival

The room is a jumble of chairs, tables and mirrors. The chairs range from bent wooden chairs to battered easy chairs, and are littered with cast-off clothes, plastic bags, scripts, half-eaten sandwiches and a regiment of empty beer cans. There are two entrances. The door upstage R leads to the corridor and the stage, and above this there hangs a battered loud speaker cabinet. Below the speaker there is a notice pinned to the wall with the words "POLDEN PLAYERS" scrawled on it. The door down L has the word "TOILET" painted on it with an arrow pointing off stage

When the CURTAIN *rises the stage is in darkness. The voice of the Adjudicator, beautifully modulated but rather scratchy, is booming away in the darkness. His speech is orchestrated with audience fidgetting noises*

Adjudicator (*off*) Now, I always say to groups who tackle this very interesting and challenging little play—always remember that in the first place you are basically dolls. Toys who emerge from a box in the attic. First a monkey with a drum, then—and dare I say it in this day and age—a gollywog ...

Titters are heard from the Audience

... a toy soldier—very stiff and correct, and then a pretty girl doll, dressed as a dancer ...

A single spot fades up to discover Sharon who resembles the very doll that the Adjudicator is describing. She is sunk in the depths of misery on a chair almost centre stage. She is in her early twenties and works in a supermarket. She has her hands over her ears and is near to tears. As the Adjudicator continues general lighting gradually fades in

These dolls come to life, but they are still dolls, and that must never be forgotten. This is not the first time I have seen this play, by any means. It seems to crop up with unfailing regularity in Festivals such as this. But I cannot recollect seeing such a performance as the ... er ... Polden Players managed tonight. To say it faltered ... er ... from time to time, would be an understatement, I fear. An understatement. But this is hardly surprising when you remember the disasters that beset these unfortunate actors. Take the girl for instance. The ... er ... doll. Was it the producer's intention to have her fall over that train set and hurl herself headlong into that toybox? Was this some bizarre new angle to this interesting little play?

There is the sound of laughter from the Audience

Joe enters UR. *He is an ebullient young man dressed as a monkey*

Joe (*vastly amused*) What a cock up! What a king-size all-time disastrous cock up! Did you see Martin? (*He takes his mask off*) Did you see him? (*He goes into peals of laughter*)

Adjudicator (*off*) So to conclude, I have to say that at this ...

Joe Ah belt up! How do you turn this thing off?

Adjudicator (*off*) ... stage of the Festival one should be prepared for anything ...

Joe gets on a chair and fiddles with the speaker

Joe I thought Martin was going to run amok. Strangle the prompt—or you—or Raymond who was flapping about in the wings like a demented fairy. (*Rattling and banging the speaker*) Ah ... shut up!

Adjudicator (*off*) But having said that, and taking everything into account, there was one performance ...

The Adjudicator's voice is cut off in mid-sentence as Joe manages to quell the speaker

Joe That's better. Gives you goose pimples listening to that berk. (*He gets off the chair*) Hey Sharon, did you see his jacket? Velvet it was. Red velvet. (*Noticing Sharon's despair*) What's up? Oh come on, you're not taking it seriously?

Sharon I made a fool of myself ... I wish I could die.

Joe What for?

Sharon I let you down. I let everybody down.

Joe Rubbish. It was just one of those nights. Furniture hurls itself
at you, prompt goes into hysterics, curtains get stuck, leading
man goes mad. One of those nights. I thought it was great. (*He
laughs and looks round for some beer and finds none*) Hey who's
pinched the beer?

Sharon (*dramatically*) I was terrible . . . terrible. I ruined the play.
I shall go and hang myself . . . in the toilet. There's nothing left.

Joe (*shaking an empty beer can*) You're right, there isn't. I reckon
those creeps from Durley have been in looting. That Stage
Manager of theirs can smell a can of beer three miles off.

Sharon What'll he say? I mean what will Raymond say?

Joe Blimey. I'm roasting in this outfit. (*He starts to peel off his
monkey skin*)

Sharon Raymond was expecting to take us to Swindon for the
Area and I've ruined it all. Oh, I could die . . .

Sharon jumps up and exits to the toilet

Joe Not in there love. Don't die in there. It's in use. Oh boy, do I
need a drink. (*He pulls the monkey skin over his head*)

Janice enters UR. *She is middle-aged and slightly flustered. She is
the prompt*

Janice Joe?

Joe (*immersed in the monkey skin*) Who's that?

Janice Have you seen Sharon?

Joe Oh it's you Janice. Come to seduce me?

Janice Not at the moment. I'm looking for Sharon.

Joe She's in there. (*He points to the toilet*) Hanging herself.

Janice Oh, good. What?

Joe Ever tried it with a monkey, Janice? 'Cause here's your
chance.

Janice (*giggling*) Oh get away! Is she all right?

Joe You're all right.

Janice Oh do be sensible. (*Slapping him away*) And keep your
hands to yourself. I thought I'd warn Sharon. Raymond's in a
terrible fury. I thought he'd slap that Adjudicator, I really did.
God knows what he'll do next.

Joe He'll get over it. Happens most years. Raymond's used to

losing ... makes a bit of a habit of it. Oh my word, Janice. I
fancy you. (*He makes another pass at her*)

Janice Get away. It's always the same with you ... every year. It
must be something you eat.

Joe (*changing his tone*) She's taking it bad. She's taking it serious.

Janice Well I'm not surprised. It put everybody off, her falling
into that box. Martin went back four pages, Chris fell over his
sword, and then Sharon dried up completely. There was nothing
left for Martin to do but jump on her and have done with it. I
couldn't do anything, couldn't even find my place. It's terrible
being a prompter in that sort of situation.

Joe Oh I enjoyed it—and so did the audience. Only belly laugh
they'd had all evening.

Janice Oh, it's all right for you, doing that monkey. Just had to
act natural.

Joe makes another pass at Janice

Ah! Stop it! I'll get my husband on to you. Proper pest you are.

Joe You shouldn't be so sexy, Janice.

*Martin bursts in. He is dressed and made-up like a gollywog. He is
in a towering rage. He glowers at Joe and marches towards the
toilet*

Sharon's in there.

Martin Blast! I'm bursting. (*He bangs on the door of the toilet*)
Hurry up ... I'm bursting.

Janice Oh, Martin. You didn't see Chris on the way up?

Martin You know she ruined my performance. Ruined it.

Joe That wouldn't be difficult.

Martin (*glowering*) Bloody comedians. (*He goes and peers at
himself in the mirror*)

Janice I can't find Chris anywhere. He seems to have vanished
into thin air. I hope he's not had an accident.

Joe He'll be in the bar if he's any sense.

Martin Bloody amateurs! I'm sick of working with amateurs! It
was like a madhouse up there, everybody falling into boxes.
How can you GIVE in that sort of shambles? (*Shouting at the
toilet*) For Pete's sake, Sharon, are you going to sit there all
night?

Joe If you're that desperate, why not go along the passage?

Martin No thank you. I'm not going to stand in there surrounded by the other groups making snide remarks.

Janice I'd better go on looking for Chris. I'm worried about him.

Joe Come back when they've all gone, Janice, and we can try it in the monkey skin.

Janice (*giggling*) Disgusting.

Janice exits

Martin She didn't help. Croaking away in the corner like a demented parrot. Oh God! Amateurs!

Joe Well you ain't no professional. The Adjudicator didn't exactly sing your praises.

Martin That reactionary creep. They should have buried him with Noël Coward. (*Shouting once more*) Come on, Sharon! There are others here you know.

Joe Go down the passage, for pete's sake.

Martin Like this?

Joe You'll be all right if you don't meet any racialists.

Martin Oh, very droll. Why do women spend hours and hours in the toilet? It's not as though it's comfortable.

Martin, now desperate, exits UR

Joe, having completed changing, starts packing his bits and pieces into a plastic bag

Joe You coming, Sharon? Or have you fallen down the plug hole?

Sharon (*emerging*) I wasn't really hiding, I was sort of . . .

Joe Seeking solitude . . . contemplating nature. I do it frequently—at work. (*He grins*) Martin had to go down the passage in his gollywog outfit.

Sharon Yes, I heard.

Joe He thinks he's a sort of superstar. Talks about amateurs as if we were bedbugs or something.

Sharon He's right, Joe. I did ruin his performance.

Joe He don't have no performance to ruin, my love. He gets up, sits down and turns at the corners, that's all.

Sharon I thought he was going to kill me in that rape bit, he was breathing so heavy.

Joe Well I'd be breathing heavy lying on the top of you.

Sharon (*exasperated*) You don't take it serious. You don't take nothing serious.

Joe Oh I dunno. I take some things serious. (*He looks at her with some meaning*) But not play-acting. I come here for a laugh. I work in a plastics factory stamping out buckets day after day, hour after hour, until a machine takes me over. So I come here for a laugh, that's all.

Sharon I want more than that. Much more.

Joe Glamour? Sex-life described in the Sunday newspapers? Third page of *The Sun*?

Sharon You know what I mean.

Joe Oh, ah. Only trouble about dreams is . . . that it ain't so good when you wake up—is it?

Sharon No it isn't. It isn't.

Joe So laugh it off, Sharon. It's only a game . . . laugh it off.

Sharon It's not so easy. You see I wanted, well I wanted to be praised, like. I mean like I was in the last round. He said I had promise. Oh why did I have to go and trip over that train set. Why? Why?

Joe Some bloody fool left it there, that's why.

Sharon I'm humiliated. (*She is near to tears*) Humiliated that's what I am . . .

Joe For pete's sake, Sharon. Face them—go in with your elbows. Bite their bloody ears.

Sharon It's not a football match, Joe.

Joe Maybe not, but I've seen better actors in football teams than you'd find amongst this lot in a month of Sundays, and that's the truth.

Martin enters

Martin (*to Joe*) You did that on purpose.

Joe What?

Martin That toilet was crammed with Durley supporters. They kept making remarks.

Joe Like "hallo Golly"?

Martin You're not funny. You're pathetic. (*He goes to his place at the dressing table and peers at himself. To Sharon*) I suppose you realize you ruined my performance.

Sharon I'm sorry, Martin.

Martin I suppose you realize I was in the running for Actor of the Year.

Joe You what?

Martin I was in the running for Actor of the Year ... for the Festival.

Joe Never. You?

Martin Yes me. It was pretty certain ... until tonight. I was thinking of turning professional. I've got more talent than this amateur rubbish can offer.

Joe (*robustly*) Crap!

Martin What?

Joe I said—crap!

Martin You don't have to be crude. Just because you're jealous.

Joe (*laughing*) Me? Jealous of you? Leave off.

Martin You're jealous ... you haven't got my talent. You're a bit player ... you'll always be a bit player.

Sharon (*trying to change the subject*) I wonder who won the trophy?

Martin (*still gazing at himself in the mirror*) I'd have been on the telly.

Joe What telly.

Martin Local telly ... They always feature the amateur Actor of the Year. I'd have been seen by millions.

Joe Oh, ah ... millions ... along with the Morris dancing team and the Mendip Bell ringers.

Martin So what? So bloody what? (*He glares at Joe*)

Joe You're up with the fairies Martin, honest to God, you're up with the fairies.

Martin How can I develop my talent with a bunch of cowboys!

Joe Oh I dunno, Clint Eastwood managed okay.

Martin Oh very funny. I'm laughing. Anyway, Clint Eastwood didn't have a clapped-out ladies hairdresser for a producer.

Joe You can't blame Raymond for being a hairdresser, any more than you can blame me for being a factory hand, or Sharon for being a shop girl or you for being a pen pusher in a bank. Because that's what we are ... and that's what we're always likely to be.

Martin (*muttering*) Bloody amateurs. (*He begins to change into his ordinary clothes*)

Joe Yes, amateurs ... when it comes to play-acting. Amateurs and there's nowt wrong with that.

Martin My whole career in ruins. I was reaching my peak. I was

beginning to tower and you have to go and fall into that bloody
box!

Sharon I'm sorry Martin. I'm real sorry . . . I didn't mean to do it.
Honest.

Joe Oh come on girl. I can't live at this altitude. I want a beer.

Sharon I can't Joe. I'm not changed.

Joe Come as you are. Nobody will mind.

Martin Bloody amateurs.

Joe You stuck in a groove or summat? Can't you say nothing else
but—bloody amateurs?

Martin Yes. Cowboys!

Joe Are you coming Sharon?

Sharon (*relenting*) Well . . .

Joe I'll buy you a shandy . . . stiffen you up. You'd be better off in
the bar than down here with Hamlet opening up his veins.

Joe takes hold of Sharon and takes her to the door

> *Raymond enters* UR. *He is middle-aged, large and rather beautiful
> and models himself on old memories of Noël Coward*

Raymond (*with arms akimbo*) Stay dear boy . . . stay. Nobody
leaves this room. (*Perambulating towards Sharon*) What happened dear? Feet too big were they?

Joe (*sharply*) Leave her alone, Raymond. She's had enough.

Raymond Haven't we all, dear boy, haven't we all.

Sharon I'm sorry Raymond. I feel awful.

Raymond Fortunes of war my dear . . . cast it aside . . . put it down
to experience. It is only *I* that am ruined. And where are you
going, may I ask?

Joe To the bar. Directly to the bar. We will not pass GO. We will
not collect two hundred pounds.

Raymond You can't, dear boy. We must all stay put until that
dreadful sadist in the velvet jacket has had his pound of flesh.
Oh my God! Did you hear what he said? Of course he was
drunk. They usually are at this stage. Has anybody seen Chris
by the way? The wretched boy has vanished.

Martin Done himself in I should hope after that shambles. What
did you want to give him a sword for? He only trips over it.

Raymond That's enough Martin. I've been ruined enough tonight.
I don't need you snapping at my heels. And where is Janice for
goodness sake?

Joe Looking for Chris.

Raymond But I am looking for Chris. Janice should be looking for me. I am the Producer. (*He sinks into a chair*) Oh heavens, why does that fearful man have to come into the dressing rooms. Absolute torture.

Joe What man?

Raymond The Adjudicator—Caligula! He's roaming the dressing-rooms like a beastly predator, and one has to be polite. One might get him again. (*To Sharon*) I'm not blaming you dear, it could happen to anyone.

Sharon I'm sorry Raymond. Things went wrong.

Martin That is the understatement of the year.

Raymond And what happened to your much vaunted "sang-froid", dear boy. Your oh so, smooth technique. You fell on that wretched girl like a beast of prey.

Martin I was trying to put some bloody life into the production.

Raymond Well you didn't have to ravish her! It was revolting.

Martin It is supposed to be revolting! It's the climax of the play.

Raymond Not according to the Adjudicator.

Martin (*with feeling*) Stuff the Adjudicator!

Raymond Well I'd like to, dear boy. Verily. But one has to be practical.

Martin I don't give a shit what the Adjudicator says. The rape scene is the climax of that play. (*He bangs his fists down on the table emphatically*)

Raymond There's no need to get excited. This isn't fringe theatre. We are not expected to expose ourselves and swear. (*He strikes his tragic posture*) Oh God, what a shambles! I have not witnessed such an unmitigated disaster since Gordon's tights split in "Wild Violets".

Martin That's just about your level—"Wild Violets".

Joe I'm going for a drink. Come on Sharon.

Raymond No! I keep telling you. Nobody leaves this room until that brute has finished gloating.

The sound of cheers and running feet can be heard, off

Great heavens! What do they think this is? A football match?

Joe (*peering out through the upstage exit*) It's that lot from Durley.

Raymond I suppose that lunatic has given them the trophy. One might have guessed.

Martin (*leaping up in a fury*) Not them. Not Durley. Not those bloody amateurs.

Raymond Yes isn't it frightful. All those geriatrics romping in their underwear.

Joe disappears through the UR *exit*

Come back, I said. Oh, God! (*He squirms down in a chair*)

Joe (*off*) Well done you guys ... it was great ... really great Carried all before you Mrs Greenwood as usual. Hey Norman ... don't get pissed tonight ... remember you've got the missus in front.

There is the sound of laughter and general conversation

Joe enters beaming and stands by the door

Raymond Do you have to make an exhibition of yourself? Haven't we suffered enough?

Joe You're turning sour Raymond. Cheer up there's always next year.

Martin (*banging the table furiously*) Durley ... Bloody Durley!

Raymond Breathe deeply dear boy.

Martin Second place to a bunch of village idiots from Durley ...

Joe Third place more likely ...

Martin (*passionately*) I'm going ... (*He jumps up*)

Raymond Not now. Not now. Do sit down Martin and stop scowling.

Martin I will not sit down. I am not going to be associated with failures! (*To Joe who is by the exit*) Move aside!

Raymond Don't be so dramatic, Martin. You always over play it. You can't go out like that. (*He indicates Martin's costume*) You look like a black militant.

Martin (*slamming back to his seat and starting to wipe off his make-up*) Actor of the Year, you said. Actor of the Year, dear boy, under my direction. Direction! You couldn't direct a piss-up in a brewery.

Raymond (*cuttingly*) It's not easy, dear boy. It's not easy to make a silk purse from a sow's ear.

Martin (*leaping up*) Do you want a smash in the face?

Joe (*enjoying himself*) Yes, go on. Have a go.

Sharon Joe!

Raymond (*giving tongue*) Fifteen years have I laboured. Fifteen years in this barren vineyard. I have taken three productions to the Area Finals. I have drunk sherry with the Mayor of Swindon. I have given myself to the Theatre. I have passed through the pain barrier in the cause of Thespus. And for what? Insults ... threats of violence, funny remarks, and protégés tearing at my throat like wild beasts. I tell you my dears—I am undone—absolutely undone. (*He beats his forehead*)

Joe I shall be undone if I don't get a pint of ale. (*He makes for the exit*)

Raymond (*writhing*) No! No!

Joe But I'm thirsty, Raymond. I'm dry. You don't know what it was like in that monkey skin. All the time I was up there ... only thing I could think about was beer.

Martin (*between his teeth*) Gordon Bennet!

Raymond I wish you wouldn't grind your teeth, Martin ... it's so unbecoming. (*A thought strikes him*) Oh damn! What the devil has happened to Chris? I don't see why he should be allowed to escape.

Sharon I think his mother was out front.

Raymond I doubt if he has one, dear.

Martin leaps up and makes for the exit. He has now removed his make-up and is more or less changed

Martin Well, that's it!

Raymond (*brandishing his arms*) No stay, dear boy. We must all go down together.

Martin Not me. Dear boy! I'm going ... for good! You're rubbish ... all of you ... Rubbish. It's people like you who give the theatre a bad name!

Martin rushes towards the exit. Joe puts a foot out and trips him

(*Waving his fists*) Ignorant thug!

Joe Temper ... temper.

Martin exits in a rage

Raymond Oh damn! Now I shall have to pacify him. I wish you wouldn't do things like that Joe, we're not on the football terraces.

Joe He called us rubbish.

Raymond I know ... but juvenile leads don't grow on trees. Young lovers are hard to come by.

Joe (*grinning meaningfully*) Are they? I didn't know.

Raymond (*after pouting and scowling in answer to Joe*) I'd better go after him. He'll only bitch all over the theatre. I suppose Chris is falling down drunk in the bar with Janice and the rest of them. God what a shambles!

Joe We'll come with you.

Raymond Oh no you won't. You'll stay here. And you Sharon. Somebody has to be fed to that beast in the velvet jacket. Oh God! I feel like Napoleon after Waterloo. (*He moves towards the exit* R. *To Sharon*) It wasn't so much the train dear. But you fell into the box. It's very difficult to recover from that sort of situation.

Raymond exits

(*Off*) Martin! Stay dear boy. Stay. All is forgiven ... (*His voice drifts away down the corridor*)

Sharon rushes into the toilet

Joe Well I like that. If he thinks we're going to stop here just for ... (*He turns to continue his conversation with Sharon*) Where the heck? (*He glances towards the toilet*) Oh no ... not again. (*He goes to the toilet door and shouts*) You in there Sharon?

Sharon (*off*) Go away.

Joe Don't be daft! You're not doing yourself any good. And you don't want to pay any attention to Raymond ... nobody else does. Open the door and let me in. (*He changes tack*) It's no good hiding, Sharon. Creeping into a hole like a little mouse because some guy in a velvet jacket criticises you. That's not going to win friends and influence people. (*Still getting no reply*) All right then, stay there. You can speak to the Adjudicator through the door when he comes. I'm going for a beer. Bye ...

Joe stamps towards the UR *exit, making as much noise as possible*

Sharon emerges from the toilet

Sharon (*pathetically*) Don't leave me Joe, please ...

Joe There's hardly room for two in there. I mean we'd be a bit pressed for space, but if that's what you want.

Sharon Please be serious Joe. I wasn't no good, and everybody knows it.

Joe Rubbish ... you were marvellous and you could act the pants off the lot of them.

Sharon Think so?

Joe (*with feeling*) Know so.

Sharon (*smiling*) Liar.

Joe No ... no ... that's the truth and I am being serious.

Sharon What about Martin? What about Raymond? What about the Adjudicator? I don't suppose they'd agree with you.

Joe Comics, girl. Comedians who strut and fret their hour upon the stage and then are heard no more. (*Surprised at his own lucidity*) How about that? ... I've got culture. Tell I've been to evening classes.

Sharon (*coming to a decision*) I can't come like this. I'll have to change.

Joe (*taking a chair*) Great! I'll watch you.

Sharon Pardon?

Joe I'll watch ... I like seeing pretty girls in their knickers ... and you're pretty, Sharon. You're smashing.

Sharon begins to change her clothes

Sharon I thought you preferred beer.

Joe What gave you that idea?

Sharon You ain't stopped going on about pints since you came in.

Joe It's a question of priority. (*He looks at her admiringly*)

Sharon Do you fancy me? Joe.

Joe What?

Sharon (*flauntingly*) Like to see my birth mark?

Joe Yes please.

Sharon (*giggling*) I ain't got one. (*She continues to dress*)

Joe Watch out! I've got wandering hands. Ask Janice.

Sharon Do you really think I'm good, Joe. As an actress.

Joe Oh yes. Very good ...

Sharon (*now almost completely dressed*) Be serious.

Joe I think you're seriously smashing. In every way.

Sharon And I think you're smashing, in every way. (*She puts her arms round him*)

Joe Hey, steady on.

Sharon No ... I think you're smashing because you make me feel

good. And you're a smashing gorilla . . . and you took my side
against the others . . . and I think you're nice and cuddly and
smashing and . . . (*They start to kiss and cuddle*)

Janice pokes her head round the upstage door

Janice Oh . . . I beg your pardon. (*She starts to go then sees it is
Joe and Sharon*) Oh it's you Joe. Don't you ever get tired.
Joe It's the tablets Jan . . . I keep taking them.
Janice Yes. Oh well. Chris hasn't been down here, has he?
Joe Not that I know of. I haven't forsaken you, this is just a bit on
the side.
Sharon Don't listen to him, Janice. He's a liar.
Janice Oh I know that, Sharon. If you see Chris, will you tell him
his mother is looking for him. Tell him we're all looking for him.
I can't think where he could have got to. I've looked in the bar
and all the dressing rooms. I do hope he hasn't stabbed himself
with his sword. I seem to spend all my time looking for people
who aren't there . . . It's very confusing.

Janice exits

Sharon You shouldn't have said that Joe.
Joe What?
Sharon About having a bit on the side. I don't know what she'll
think.
Joe Oh she's used to it. I attack her every year . . . it keeps me in
trim.
Sharon You're not married are you Joe?
Joe No. Why?
Sharon Oh, nothing. Hey . . . do you think it would work? With
other people . . . other guys?
Joe What?
Sharon (*vamping*) What I done to you.
Joe You don't know what you've done to me.
Sharon Don't I?
Joe (*breaking away*) I need a beer. Oh boy do I need a beer.
Sharon (*with startling conviction*) I'd sell myself, Joe. To be an
actress. To get away from . . . I'd sell myself.
Joe Would you?
Sharon You don't know what it's like . . . where I come from.
Joe Oh yes I do. I do.

Sharon It's so boring. It's so deadly boring. There's nothing . . . nothing except this drama club.

Joe We're all in the same boat, you know. All trying to get out. Some of us do. Most of us don't. Got to make the best of it . . . have a bit of a laugh and a pint. Got to make the best of it.

Sharon I want to be famous. I want to be somebody. I'm fed up with being a statistic, I want to be notable. Stand out of the crowd.

Joe You stand out of the crowd all right.

Sharon Do I?

Joe In my book you do. Greatly. Tell you what let's go back to my place and talk it over.

Sharon (*nettled*) Can't you ever be serious?

Joe Better laugh than cry . . . that's what I say. (*He picks up Martin's wig*) Well we're only a bunch of cowboys . . . (*He puts the wig on and imitates Martin*) Amateurs . . . Bloody amateurs. How can I give myself . . . How can I tower . . . How can I exercise my talents with a bunch of Amateurs! (*He pirouettes in an extravagant imitation of Martin mixed with Raymond*)

The Adjudicator enters UR

Adjudicator Good evening.

Joe Oh . . . ah . . .

Adjudicator (*consulting his notes*) So you're the Gollywog?

Joe Pardon?

Adjudicator (*consulting his notes again*) This is . . . er . . . (*He peers at the notice on the wall*) Yes, it is . . .

Janice rushes in UR

Janice Watch out Joe—he's coming . . . (*She freezes at the sight of the Adjudicator*) Hullo.

Adjudicator Hullo . . . I expect you're the Producer.

Janice Pardon?

Adjudicator (*valiantly; to Joe*) I don't expect you intended to fall on her quite so determinedly . . .

Joe What?

Adjudicator Of course I always think that tremendous symbolic finalé should be gone into very carefully . . . very carefully indeed. You see Black Africa . . .

Joe I was the monkey.

Adjudicator Oh ... What?

Joe I was the monkey ... the one with the drum ...

Adjudicator Oh good heavens ... Yes of course ... I should have recognized you ... (*He laughs weakly*)

Janice I think he went down the passage.

Adjudicator Who?

Janice Black Africa.

Adjudicator Really? (*He smiles wanly*) You made a valiant effort you know ... I liked your diagonals, such as they were.

Janice My what?

Adjudicator You are the Producer?

Janice No, I'm the prompt.

The Adjudicator passes his hand across his brow

We are looking for the Producer.

Adjudicator (*confused*) Really? (*He sees Sharon who is hiding behind Joe*) Hullo there ... I think I know what part you played ...

Sharon (*despairingly*) No!

Adjudicator What?

Sharon No ... (*She shakes her head, near to tears*)

Adjudicator (*again confused; turning to Joe*) Staccato ... that's the secret. It's symbolic you know ... and deeply sexual.

Joe Pardon?

Adjudicator The drum ... your drum ... It's deeply sexual, have you thought of that.

Joe Er ... no.

Adjudicator They never do, you know ... they never do. The key to this play is the vibrating sexuality of the monkey's drum. It pulsates with phallic symbolism ... don't you see?

Joe does not see and therefore cannot think of any reply

Keep banging away ... just keep banging away. (*To Sharon*) Of course I know what part you played ... Oh dear, oh dear ... what a pity.

Joe (*aggressively*) She was good.

Adjudicator Undeniably.

Joe And it wasn't her fault that she fell into the box ... it could happen to anyone.

Adjudicator Yes indeed ...

Joe So just go easy ... go easy ... What did you say?

Adjudicator I said yes indeed.

Joe Before that ...

Adjudicator Before what?

Joe You said ... Undeniably.

Adjudicator Oh yes ... (*He shakes his head*) But it is such a pity ...

Joe Oh blimey!

Adjudicator It is such a pity that you were not, as it were, in the body of the hall, when I made the announcement.

Joe What announcement? What announcement?

Adjudicator I would have thought that it might have come to you over the speaker. I rather pride myself on a full rich voice and clear enunciation. You see taking all things into consideration and in the face of quite considerable promise ... I ... er ... named you as Performer of the Year for the Festival ... er ... congratulations. (*He fishes in his folder and produces a parchment*) Jolly good show.

There is a stunned silence. The Adjudicator places the parchment on the make-up table

A most interesting and ... er ... vibrating performance. (*He laughs languidly. To Joe*) Keep banging away ... keep banging away ... Now then ... (*He moves towards the exit*) The Durley Players ... I believe. Does one know where they are?

Janice (*coming out of her daze*) Yes ... yes ... next door ... (*She goes to the door and directs the Adjudicator on his way*)

The Adjudicator exits

Joe Oh boy. Oh boy. Just wait till I see Martin. (*He rolls about choking with laughter*) I can't wait ... I can't bloody wait!

Sharon I don't believe it. I just don't believe it.

Joe I told you girl. I told you—that one's no fool, velvet jacket and all ... Ta rah! Sharon Peabody ... Actor of the year ... or should it be Actress? ... Ta rah! Ta rah!

Sharon I don't believe it.

Joe grabs Sharon and twirls her round

Oh put me down Joe ... you're making me giddy.

Janice enters

Janice Well I never . . . I never . . .

Joe I know you never, Janice. But I keep trying. (*He abandons Sharon for a moment and makes a pass at Janice*)

Janice Get off!

Sharon (*grinning*) He just keeps banging away.

Janice Congratulations Sharon, I'm so pleased for you. I really am.

Sharon You should have got Prompter of the Year, Janice. After what you've been through. (*She picks up the parchment*) I can't believe it. I just can't believe it. After making such a mess of things . . .

Joe . . . and hiding in the toilet and grovelling to Martin. Oh boy! I can't wait to see his face. Come on let's go and celebrate.

Sharon (*excitedly*) Yes . . . yes!

Joe Are you sure you want to be seen with a monkey player now that you're a star?

Sharon (*winking*) If you take your drum.

Joe I don't need no drum . . . (*He takes her hand*) . . . Not for you, Sharon.

They look at each other with a new awareness

Janice (*diplomatically*) Oh good heavens is that the time? I must fly . . . hubby will be wanting his Horlicks . . .

Raymond enters in a flap

Raymond Sanctuary! Sanctuary! Deal with her Janice for heaven's sake.

Janice Do you know what's happened to Sharon?

Raymond Later . . . later. There is a fearful woman in a "Henry Heath" hat who swears she is Chris's mother. Absolute harridan. God what a night! (*He looks round for somewhere to hide*)

A fiery woman in a felt hat appears in the doorway and moves across to the fleeing Raymond. She is Mrs Bland

Mrs Bland What have you done with him? What have you done with my poor boy?

Raymond Nothing, madam. Nothing, as God is my judge. (*He tries to get past her*) Do you mind . . . I am in need.

Mrs Bland That can wait. My boy is lost, Mr Hackworthy, and I hold you responsible.

Raymond Madam, I am not my brother's keeper. Now please leave me alone I have had a tense evening.

Janice Oh my goodness ... I've just remembered. The box!

Mrs Bland What box?

Janice I think he may be stuck in it. Oh dear ...

Mrs Bland Stuck in a box? I'll hold you responsible. (*She wags her finger at Raymond*)

Raymond Oh death where is thy sting!

Mrs Bland Don't try that theatrical stuff on with me, it won't wash. I don't trust you Mr Hackworthy. I know about hairdressers. If you have my boy in a box I shall take proceedings.

Janice If he's there it will have been a mistake Mrs Bland. The lid gets stuck.

Joe That was Martin. He slammed the lid down when he got out.

Raymond Petulant little beast.

Janice Perhaps we'd better go and see if he's there, Mrs Bland. He may need resuscitation. It gets very stuffy in that box.

Mrs Bland (*to Janice*) He's peculiar you know. He gave Mrs Green's Harold a blue rinse.

Raymond Mrs Green's Harold asked for a blue rinse madam, he's a punk rocker!

Mrs Bland I don't trust these theatricals, they're not nice. If my Chris comes out of this in one piece, he can stick to karate, and you can find another boy for your box.

Mrs Bland and Janice exit

Raymond (*flinging himself into a chair*) Monstrous female! God preserve me from militant mothers! A damnable breed. Ah well, let's hear the bad news. (*To Sharon*) What did he do to you dear? Ravish you with mixed metaphors?

Joe He gave her the Actor of the Year award.

Raymond Oh is that all? (*Sitting up*) He what?

Sharon Actor of the Year.

Raymond It should be actress, dear. Actor is masculine, though it's often hard to tell.

Joe That's what they want isn't it?

Raymond Who?

Joe The liberated woman or whatever. It's what they want.

Raymond I don't think that has anything to do with it, Joe. (*To Sharon*) Congratulations, dear. Of course I knew you'd get it.

Joe What about Martin?

Raymond That numbskull. Clodhopper, dear boy. Absolute clodhopper. You've got more talent than he has.

Joe Where is he? I want to tell him the news.

Raymond Next door.

Joe With those amateurs from Durley?

Raymond Absolutely. I saw him grovelling round that odious Mrs
Thompson their Producer. The one in the silver lamé and glass
beads. She pinches all my boys.

*Raymond puts his hand over Joe's hand who snatches it away
horrified*

Joe It must be hell for you, Raymond.

Raymond Unmitigated, dear boy. Well he's welcome to her, she's
no idea you know ... not an ounce of talent. All homemade,
tasselated tights and diagonal grouping. God knows how she
keeps on winning trophies, probably gives herself to the Adjudicator. There's a lot of bribery in this game you know. Competi-
tive drama ... pah ... it's worse than football. Killing the
theatre, my dears. Killing it. What shall we do next year? How
about *Resounding Tinkle?* Theatre of the Absurd. So it won't
matter if we make a cock-up. Oh damn it, I suppose I had better
go and see if that wretched boy has found his mother. He may
have run away to sea or something, one can hardly blame him
with that harridan running after him. I don't know how they
come to life. I really don't. (*He goes to the door*) Did that fiend
say anything about the production?

Joe He said he liked your diagonals.

Raymond Oh did he? Snide swine. They're like hanging judges.
Mad with power. Ah well, back to the grind. All those blow
dries and rinses ... and little to look forward to until *Humpty
Dumpty* in the New Year.

Raymond exits

Sharon Poor old Raymond. He's stuck too, isn't he?

Joe Yes, but he loves it. Are you ready, Miss Peabody, to meet
your clamouring fans?

Sharon I'm ready for anything. (*She takes his hand*) Anything.

Joe Oh boy. Let's start with a pint then ...

Singing can be heard off "We won the cup, we won the cup" etc.

Joe (*performing an exaggerated imitation of Raymond*) It's worse than football. Killing the theatre, my dears. Just killing the theatre.

Joe and Sharon exit hand in hand as the Lights fade, and the singing increases in volume

CURTAIN

FURNITURE AND PROPERTY LIST

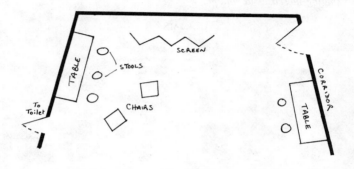

On stage: Tables. Above them: mirrors and bare light bulbs (optional)
Screen (optional)
Stools
Various chairs
Loudspeaker cabinet on wall
Notices on walls—"Polden Players" and "Toilet"
Cast-off clothes (changes for the cast)
Plastic bags
Scripts
Half-eaten sandwiches
Empty beer cans
Make-up
Other dressing as required

Personal: **Adjudicator:** Folder with parchment inside for "Performer of the Year"

EFFECTS PLOT

Cue 1   As Curtain rises   (Page 1)
Recording of Adjudicator's speech, with accompanying Audience noises, coming through the dressing-room speakers. See text pp. 1–2

Cue 2   **Adjudicator:** "... there was one performance ..."   (Page 2)
Cut recording as Joe switches speakers off

Cue 3   **Raymond:** "... brute has finished gloating."   (Page 9)
Running feet and cheering

Cue 4   **Joe:** "... you've got the missus in front."   (Page 10)
Laughter and general conversation

Cue 5   **Joe:** "Let's start with a pint then ..."   (Page 20)
Singing: "We Won The Cup" etc

LIGHTING PLOT

Property fittings required: centre light. Practical fittings required: bare bulbs above mirrors (optional)

A dressing room.

To open: Black-out

Cue 1   **Adjudicator's voice:** "... dressed as a dancer ..."   (Page 1)
              Single spot fades up on **Sharon**. *Gradually fade in general lighting*

Cue 2   **Joe:** "Just killing the theatre."   (Page 21)
              Lights fade to Black-out

MADE AND PRINTED IN GREAT BRITAIN BY
LATIMER TREND & COMPANY LTD PLYMOUTH

MADE IN ENGLAND